SPRING

Phonemic Awareness Songs & Rhymes

♪ Fun Lyrics Sung to Familiar Tunes ♫

D0730972

• Written by •

Kimberly Jordano & Trisha Callella-Jones

Editor: Kristine Johnson

Illustrator: Darcy Tom

Project Director: Carolea Williams

Table of Contents

Introduction

Before children learn to read words in print, they must develop the important skill of auditory discrimination—an awareness of how letters and words are used in oral language. *Phonemic Awareness Songs & Rhymes* provides theme-related songs and activities that encourage children to manipulate sounds and "play with language." Children learn to

- *listen for and identify rhyming words.*
- *identify words that include the same sound.*
- *listen for and count syllables within a word.*
- *identify the beginning, middle, and ending sounds in words.*
- *count and clap out the number of sounds in words.*
- *combine letter sounds to form words.*
- *divide words into separate sounds.*
- *match sounds to letters of the alphabet.*

The activities and songs in this resource are both easy to use and fun to do. Each reproducible activity card and song sheet clearly identifies the phonemic-awareness task(s) being reinforced. The cards and song sheets also indicate which songs and activities can be taught together. *Phonemic Awareness Songs & Rhymes* also includes supplementary reproducibles and a helpful cross-check index to simplify lesson preparations. If you are unfamiliar with any of the tunes, simply chant the song as a rhyme. This is an all-in-one resource filled with fun, interactive activities and silly, playful songs—a winning combination for any reading-development program!

What Is Phonemic Awareness?

Phonemic awareness is the ability to recognize and manipulate individual sound units (phonemes) in spoken language: to examine language independent of meaning, to see relationships between sounds in words, and to rearrange sounds to create new words. For example, the word *chick* is made up of three phonemes (/ch/ /i/ /k/*); it can be changed to the word *pick* by replacing /ch/ with /p/.

Students who are phonemically aware are able to master the following tasks:

Rhyming—The ability to identify and form rhyming words.

 Example: Do these words rhyme?

    fun—fan *no*

    pig—wig *yes*

    cheer—year *yes*

    bread—seed *no*

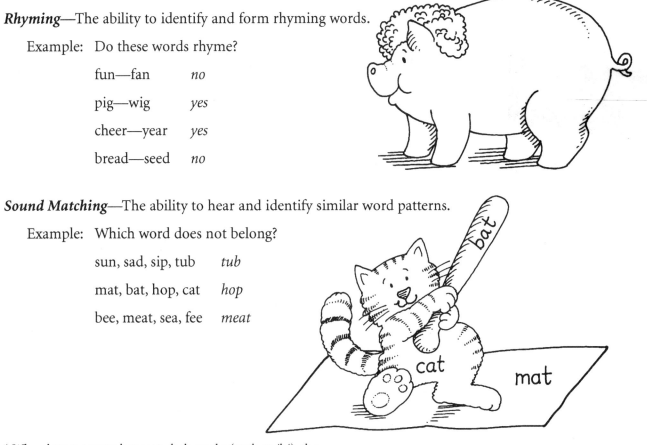

Sound Matching—The ability to hear and identify similar word patterns.

 Example: Which word does not belong?

    sun, sad, sip, tub *tub*

    mat, bat, hop, cat *hop*

    bee, meat, sea, fee *meat*

* When letters appear between slash marks (such as /k/), the sound rather than the letter name is represented.

Syllable Counting—The ability to identify the number of syllables in spoken words.

Example: How many syllables do you hear in these words?

ticket	*2*
dog	*1*
bicycle	*3*
pencil	*2*

Syllable Splitting—The ability to identify onsets and rimes.*

Example: What word do you have when you join these sounds together?

j–ump	*jump*
t–an	*tan*
cl–imb	*climb*
str–eet	*street*

Phoneme Blending—The ability to orally blend individual sounds to form a word.

Example: What word do you have when you join these sounds together?

/m/ /a/ /p/	*map*
/j/ /a/ /k/	*jack*
/ch/ /ee/ /p/	*cheap*
/b/ /r/ /o/ /k/	*broke*

* An *onset* is all the sounds in a word that come before the first vowel. A *rime* is the first vowel in a word and all the sounds that follow. (For example, in the word *splash,* the onset is *spl-* and the rime is *-ash.*)

Phoneme Isolation—The ability to identify the beginning, middle, and ending sounds in a word.

Examples:

What's the beginning sound in *toe?*   /t/

What's the middle sound in *big?*   /i/

What's the ending sound in *plane?*   /n/

There are four sounds in "treat."

Phoneme Counting—The ability to count the number of phonemes in a word.

Example: How many sounds do you hear in these words?

at   2

lake   3

paint   4

tent   4

Phoneme Segmentation—The ability to break apart a word into individual sounds.

Example: Which sounds do you hear in these words?

mud   /m/ /u/ /d/

play   /p/ /l/ /a/

strike   /s/ /t/ /r/ /i/ /k/

Mud!
/m/ /u/ /d/

Phoneme Addition—The ability to add a beginning, middle, or ending sound to a word.

Examples:

$$p + lay = play$$
$$grew + m = groom$$

What word would you have if you added /b/ to the beginning of *low*? *blow*

What word would you have if you added /r/ to the middle of *bed*? *bread*

What word would you have if you added /s/ to the end of *how*? *house*

Phoneme Deletion—The ability to omit the beginning, middle, or ending sound from a word.

Examples:

What word would you have if you took out the /f/ in *flake*? *lake*

What word would you have if you took out the /l/ in *play*? *pay*

What word would you have if you took out the /t/ in *meat*? *me*

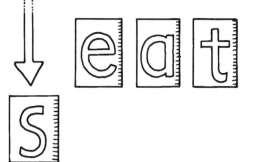

Phoneme Substitution—The ability to substitute a new sound for the beginning, middle, or ending sound of a word.

Examples:

What word would you have if you changed the /b/ in *ball* to a /t/? *tall*

What word would you have if you changed the /o/ in *hot* to an /a/? *hat*

What word would you have if you changed the /p/ in *map* to a /d/? *mad*

Make the Most of It!

The songs and rhymes in this resource help lay a foundation for phonics instruction in a fun and exciting way. Use them when teaching specific phonemic-awareness tasks (see the song titles listed on individual activity cards), or follow the suggestions below to incorporate these "kid-captivating" songs and rhymes into your core curriculum.

Song Cards

Enlarge, decorate, and laminate each song for daily shared reading and singing. Use "magic wands" or theme-related reading sticks to point to the words as students sing the songs. Make a fun, accessible display by using clothespins to hang the song sheets from a plastic toy chain, or store the song sheets in baskets for use at a center or for free-choice reading time.

Individual Songbooks

Provide each student with a three-pronged folder. As a new song is learned, give each child a photocopy of the song sheet to decorate, read, sing, and then add to his or her notebook. Provide weekly opportunities for students to reread and sing their favorite songs. Send the notebooks home at Open House or at the end of the year for students to share with their families.

Songs on Tape

Practice singing the songs with your students. Once students are familiar with a song, use a tape recorder to make a class tape of the song. Place copies of the song sheets and the cassette at a listening center for students to use.

Farm Animals

I see some animals
  little and big,
A rooster, a turkey,
  and a pig.
But the one on the farm
That rhymes with [now]
Is my favorite.
It's the ☐.

Charts

Copy the songs onto large individual sheets of chart paper. Use different colored markers to write key words or sounds. Invite students to "frame" the key words with their hands or with Wikki Stix (available at teacher-supply stores), use a reading stick to point to the words, highlight key words with highlighters or highlighting tape (found at most office-supply stores), or cover words with sticky notes. For additional learning and fun, add to the chart related pictures or reproducible picture cards from the back of this resource.

Big Books

Write each line from one of the songs on a separate sheet of large construction paper. Invite students to draw pictures on the construction paper that correspond to each line. Bind pages into a class big book and display it in the class library for students to reread.

I'm a little green frog, sitting in the water.

Photo Name Cards

Take a photograph of each child and of any classroom pets or puppets. Write each student's name on an index card, a sentence strip, or a tongue depressor, and then attach his or her photo to it. Place the photo name cards in a pocket chart or hold them up while you sing name-recognition songs.

Puppets

Make reduced copies of a song sheet, glue them to the backs of individual paper lunch sacks, and distribute them to students. Have students draw favorite song-related characters on the front of their sack to make paper-sack puppets. Invite the class to use the hand puppets while singing and dramatizing the corresponding song written on the back.

Flannel Board

Cover the song lyrics on the song sheet with paper, photocopy the song-sheet artwork onto card stock, and color the images. Photocopy any picture cards from the back of this resource that correspond to the song, cut them out, and color them. Invite students to draw pictures that correspond to the song, and then photocopy the pictures onto card stock. Glue felt or attach Velcro to the back of the card stock. Invite students to manipulate the images on a flannel board while singing the song.

Magnetic Board

Magnetic boards include cookie sheets, oven-burner covers, and magnetic chalk-boards. Photocopy on card stock picture cards from the back of this resource, cut them out, and color them. Write song lyrics on sentence strips and alphabet letters on index cards. Add magnetic tape to the backs of the sentence strips, picture cards, and letter cards. Invite students to manipulate the images or letters on the magnetic board while singing the song.

Storyboards

Invite students to create a construction-paper backdrop that represents a scene from a song. Have students draw pictures, cut them out, and glue some of them directly on the backdrop to make a storyboard. Invite students to glue other pictures to craft sticks to be used as pointers or puppets while singing.

Music and Movement

March around the room with students while singing one of the songs. For extra fun, give students pom-poms and/or musical instruments to use while they sing. Ask a volunteer to "be the teacher" and point to each word on the song chart. Allow students to sing solos or duets in front of the class.

Themes and Topics

Enrich your studies by placing a copy of the song sheet on the back of theme-related projects, bulletin boards, illustrated wall stories, artwork, or class big books. Use the songs to introduce new units and to generate ideas for artwork.

Card Sorting

Place in a pocket chart picture cards from the back of this resource. Invite students to sort the picture cards by various categories, such as initial sound, final sound, rhyming pairs, number of sounds, or number of syllables. For additional learning, place the picture cards in a learning center for students to re-sort.

Rhyming March

Have students place their chairs in a circle. Place on the chairs picture cards from the back of this resource, and then have students march around the chairs while singing one of the songs. When the music stops, have students say a word that rhymes with the picture card next to them. Remind students that rhyming words can be nonsense words, too.

Reading Strategies

Write the lines of one of the songs on sentence strips and distribute them to different students. Also distribute any picture cards from the back of this resource if they correspond with the song. While singing the song, invite students to place their sentence strip or picture card in the appropriate place in the pocket chart. Prompt students with reading-strategy questions such as

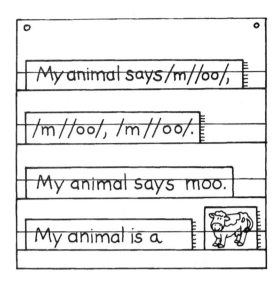

What sound do you hear at the beginning of _____? What letter do you expect to see? Does that make sense, sound right, and look right? What would the first letter of the sentence look like? What do you expect to see at the end of the sentence? How many letters are in the word _____? How many words are in the sentence?

It starts with /sh/
And it rhymes with bark.
We might see a shark!

Sentence Manipulation

Write the lines of a song on sentence strips and then cut apart the strips into words or phrases. Write some consonants on index cards for students to substitute different phonemes. Invite students to rebuild or manipulate the song.

Jump Rope Chants

Invite students to jump rope or bounce a ball while chanting the songs. The steady beat of the jump rope will help children keep the rhyming pattern. Challenge students to continue jumping rope or bouncing the ball throughout an entire song.

This little bee sings /b/ songs. He sings /b/ songs all day long.

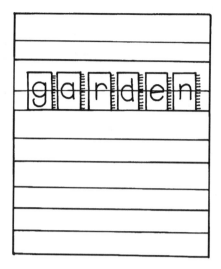

Unscramble the Word

Print in large letters on a sentence strip a key word from one of the songs. Cut apart the letters, and pass out each letter to a different student. Invite students to bring their letter to the pocket chart and reassemble the word.

Be the Word

Write letters on separate index cards and distribute the cards to students. Call out a word from a song and invite students who have a letter from that word to stand in the correct order to "be," or rebuild, the word. To "be" the sentence, write words from a song on separate index cards and pass them out. Have students stand in the correct order to rebuild the sentence.

Word Families

Use magnetic letters on a magnetic surface to spell a common rhyming word, such as cat. Invite students to replace the first letter of the word with another to form additional rhyming words, such as bat, hat, and sat. Extend learning by having students spell out high-frequency words used in the song lyrics.

Magic Reading Sticks

To make reading sticks for pointing to song lyrics while chanting or singing, have students dip the ends of chopsticks into brightly colored paint and sprinkle them with glitter. Invite students to tie ribbons to their "magical" reading stick. Create more reading sticks by using a hot glue gun to attach to dowels plastic animals or other small toys that correspond with subjects in the songs.

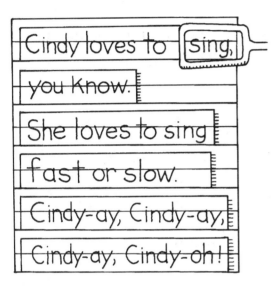

Word Hunts

Cut out a rectangular hole in the center of several brightly colored flyswatters so that when the flyswatters are placed over a word on a chart or a sentence strip, the word is framed. (Cut some holes longer than others so different-size words can be framed.) Invite a student to come to a chart or pocket chart and "hunt" for a word. For example, have a student hunt for a word that rhymes with *ring* and begins with /s/. The student then frames the word *sing* using the flyswatter.

Magic Reading Glasses

Collect inexpensive plastic toy glasses (available at party-supply stores), and punch out the lenses. Add curling ribbon to the sides of each pair for a fun decoration. Place the glasses in a special place for students to wear while reading.

Very Special Visors

Collect a few plastic visors. Decorate the visors with puffy paint and glitter glue. Invite a "leader of the day" to wear the visor and choose a favorite song for the class to sing.

♫ Down in My Garden ♫

(sing to the tune of "You Are My Sunshine")

Down in my garden,

My lovely garden.

So many pretty plants will grow.

Tell me which one is my favorite.

Say the plant name very slow.

dai—sy

Note: Hold up a picture of a plant and have students separate the sounds of the plant's name into syllables or phonemes.

Additional verses: Replace the bolded word with other plant names. Have students divide the new words into syllables, or give isolated phonemes for students to blend. For example, *Say the plant name very slow. /r/ /o/ /z/*

I've Been Working in My Garden

(sing to the tune of "I've Been Working on the Railroad")

I've been working in my garden
On this beautiful day.
I've been working in my garden
Just to pass the time away.
I can see a plant growing.
It begins with the sound **/k/.**
I can see a plant growing.
Is it **onion, lettuce,** or **corn?**

/k/ /k/ corn
/k/ /k/ corn
I see some **corn** growing.
/k/ /k/ corn
/k/ /k/ corn
I will have some **corn.**

I've been working in my garden
On this beautiful day.
I've been working in my garden
Just to pass the time away.
I can see a plant growing.
It ends with the sound **/p/.**
I can see a plant growing.
Is it **potato, turnip,** or **squash?**

Turnip /p/ /p/
Turnip /p/ /p/
I see a **turnip** growing.
Turnip /p/ /p/
Turnip /p/ /p/
I will have a **turnip.**

Additional verses: Replace bolded phonemes and words to continue the song.
For example, */b/ /b/ beets. /b/ /b/ beets. I see some **beets** growing.*

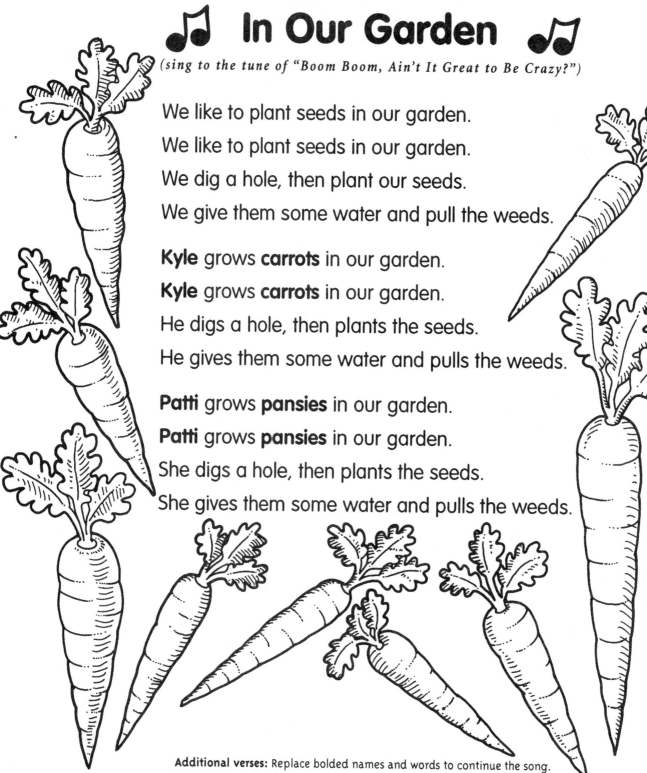

♫ In Our Garden ♫

(sing to the tune of "Boom Boom, Ain't It Great to Be Crazy?")

We like to plant seeds in our garden.

We like to plant seeds in our garden.

We dig a hole, then plant our seeds.

We give them some water and pull the weeds.

Kyle grows **carrots** in our garden.

Kyle grows **carrots** in our garden.

He digs a hole, then plants the seeds.

He gives them some water and pulls the weeds.

Patti grows **pansies** in our garden.

Patti grows **pansies** in our garden.

She digs a hole, then plants the seeds.

She gives them some water and pulls the weeds.

Additional verses: Replace bolded names and words to continue the song. For example, *Mikayla* grows *mangoes* in our garden.

Spring Phonemic Awareness Songs & Rhymes © 1998 Creative Teaching Press

See What Grows in My Garden

(sing to the tune of "For He's a Jolly Good Fellow")

See what grows in my garden.
See what grows in my garden.
See what grows in my garden.
Make a word that rhymes with **showers.**

See what grows in my garden.
See what grows in my garden.
See what grows in my garden.
Make a word that rhymes with **horn.**

See what grows in my garden.
See what grows in my garden.
See what grows in my garden.
Make a word that rhymes with **seeds.**

Note: Have students respond with a rhyming word after each stanza.
Additional verses: Replace bolded words to continue the song. For example,
*Make a word that rhymes with **bees.***

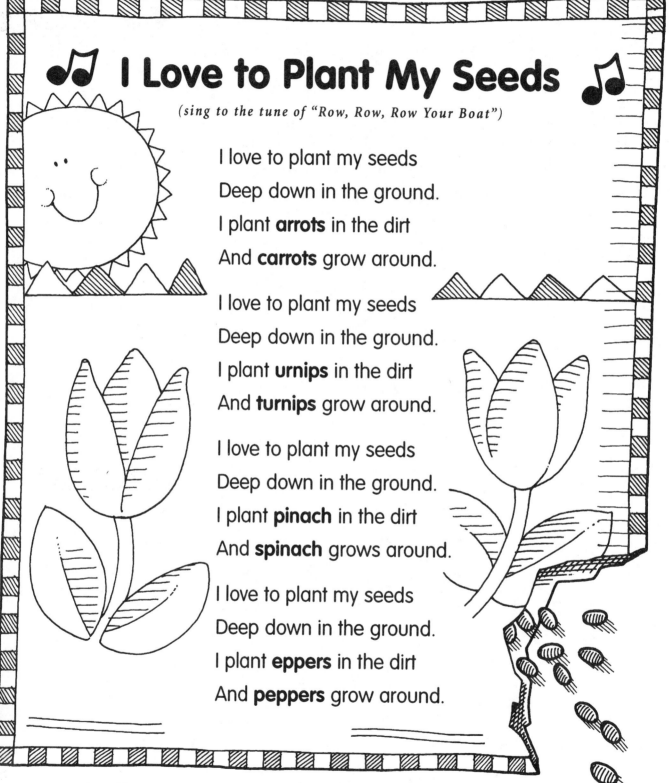

♫ I Love to Plant My Seeds

(sing to the tune of "Row, Row, Row Your Boat")

I love to plant my seeds
Deep down in the ground.
I plant **arrots** in the dirt
And **carrots** grow around.

I love to plant my seeds
Deep down in the ground.
I plant **urnips** in the dirt
And **turnips** grow around.

I love to plant my seeds
Deep down in the ground.
I plant **pinach** in the dirt
And **spinach** grows around.

I love to plant my seeds
Deep down in the ground.
I plant **eppers** in the dirt
And **peppers** grow around.

Additional verses: Replace bolded words to continue the song. Delete the first sound and pause for students to complete the word. For example, *I plant **lowers** in the dirt and **flowers** grow around.*

Spring Phonemic Awareness Songs & Rhymes © 1998 Creative Teaching Press

From the Garden

Sound Matching, Phoneme Blending, Phoneme Segmentation

Place fruits, vegetables, or flowers in a plastic flower pot or grocery sack. Invite one student to be the "sounder" and another to be the "matcher." Have the sounder secretly choose an item from the flower pot or sack and without touching it, say the first sound of the item. The matcher holds up an item from the flower pot that starts with the same sound. If that item was not the item the sounder chose, the sounder says the first and second sounds of that item. Continue until the matcher holds up the correct item. Continue playing with another set of students.

(Use with "Down in My Garden," page 16)

Materials

- plastic flower pot or grocery sack

- fruits, vegetables, and/or flowers (plastic or real)

Garden Time

Syllable Counting

Number four index cards 1–4 (one number per card). Place masking tape on the floor in four columns to make a graph. Tape an index card at the top of each column. Give students plastic or real fruits, vegetables, and flowers. Have them sort the items on the floor graph by the number of syllables in each word.

(Use with "Down in My Garden," page 16)

Materials

- 4 index cards

- masking tape

- fruits, vegetables, and flowers (plastic or real)

Guess My Seed
Phoneme Isolation

Materials

● "I've Been Working in My Garden" song (page 17)

● glue or tape

● vegetable seed packets

● craft sticks

Glue or tape seed packets to craft sticks. Call several students to stand in front of the class and distribute a packet to each, but have them turn the picture away from the class. Sing "I've Been Working in My Garden" with the class and give the initial or final sound clue and choices. Ask the student with the packet representing the correct choice to reveal the front of the seed packet and step out of line while the class sings the verse.

(Use with "I've Been Working in My Garden," page 17)

The Bunny Hop
Sound Matching, Syllable Counting

Materials

● bunny ears

● vegetables or pictures of vegetables

Have students sit in a circle. Choose one student to be the "bunny" and another to be the "farmer." Place vegetables or vegetable pictures in the middle of the circle. The bunny wears bunny ears and says *Feed me something that begins with (sound name)*. The farmer finds a vegetable that has the same initial sound and says its name. For example, if the bunny said *Feed me something that begins with /k/*, the farmer would look at the vegetables, hold up a carrot, and say *Carrots!* The bunny answers *How many hops do I get?* The class then claps the syllables in the word *carrots*. The bunny takes two hops and then joins the circle. Continue the game with a new bunny and farmer until all vegetables have been selected.

(Use with "I've Been Working in My Garden," page 17)

Great Gardeners Class Book
Sound Matching

Have each child illustrate a copy of the Seed Package reproducible and complete the frame *(Student's name) grows (plant name) in the garden*. Have students choose a plant name that begins with the same sound as their name. For example, **Kessler** *grows* **kiwi** *in the garden* or **Daniel** *grows* **daisies** *in the garden*. Bind the pages together and title the book *Our Classroom Collection of Great Gardeners*.

(Use with "In Our Garden," page 18)

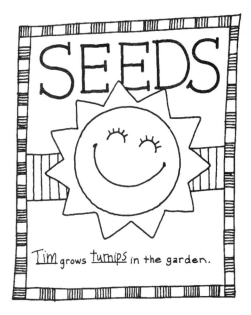

Materials

- Seed Package reproducible (page 86)
- crayons or markers
- bookbinding materials

Garden Mural Matching
Sound Matching

In advance, make letter cards by writing each letter of the alphabet on a separate index card. Have students brainstorm fruits and vegetables they would like to show in a garden mural. Invite students to paint items from the list on butcher paper in the form of a giant garden mural. When the paint dries, have students tape or tack letter cards next to garden items that begin with the same sound.

(Use with "In Our Garden," page 18)

Materials

- index cards
- paint and paintbrushes
- butcher paper
- tape or tacks

How Does Your Garden Grow?

Rhyming

Draw a background of a garden including dirt, grass, etc. on the board. Sing "See What Grows in My Garden" with your class. When the class sings the rhyming word for what grows in your garden, invite a child to come up and draw the picture on your garden mural. After singing the song, divide the class

into small groups. Challenge each group to create their own version of the song and draw on construction paper their rhyming word. Invite each group to sing their stanza and have the rest of the class say the rhyme. Then have the group show their picture and add it to the mural.

(Use with "See What Grows in My Garden," page 19)

Materials

- "See What Grows in My Garden" song (page 19)

- chalkboard

- colored chalk

- construction paper

- crayons or markers

Our Garden Rhyming Book

Rhyming

Have pairs of students draw a picture that incorporates a pair of rhyming words from "See What Grows in My Garden." Then have them write (or dictate for you to write) a sentence describing the scene. For example, *I wash the squash.*

(Use with "See What Grows in My Garden," page 19)

Materials

- "See What Grows in My Garden" song (page 19)

- construction paper

- crayons or markers

The showers grow flowers.

Let's Make a Word!

Phoneme Addition, Phoneme Substitution

Write on index cards different plant names with the onset (beginning sound) deleted and place them in a pocket chart. Write the missing onsets on separate index cards and place them in the pocket chart. As the class sings "I Love to Plant My Seeds," invite a student to find the missing beginning sound and place that letter card in front of the word. Continue with other words. For additional practice, invite students to substitute the beginning sound with different sounds to create rhyming words. For example, after making the word *carrots*, the students could replace the *c* with *p*, *l*, or *z* to make *parrots*, *larrots*, or *zarrots*.

(Use with "I Love to Plant My Seeds," page 20)

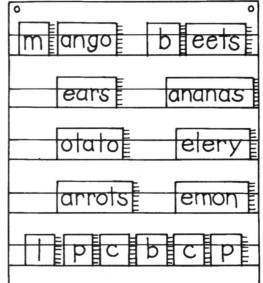

Materials

- "I Love to Plant My Seeds" song (page 20)
- index cards
- pocket chart

Plant a Letter

Phoneme Addition, Phoneme Deletion

Invite students to act out planting seeds in a garden while singing "I Love to Plant My Seeds." Then ask a student to suggest the name of a fruit or vegetable that will be planted next, but have the student delete the first sound. The rest of the class must add the missing first sound to continue the song.

(Use with "I Love to Plant My Seeds," page 20)

Materials

- "I Love to Plant My Seeds" song (page 20)

♫ On Our Farm ♫

(sing to the tune of "Old MacDonald Had a Farm")

The _____ class had a farm. E-I-E-I-O.

And on that farm we had a **pig**. E-I-E-I-O.

With a **poink poink** here,

And a **poink poink** there.

Here a **poink**. There a **poink**.

Everywhere a **poink poink**.

The _____ class had a **pig**. E-I-E-I-O.

The _____ class had a farm. E-I-E-I-O.

And on that farm we had a **cow**. E-I-E-I-O.

With a **coo coo** here,

And a **coo coo** there.

Here a **coo**. There a **coo**.

Everywhere a **coo coo**.

The _____ class had a **cow**. E-I-E-I-O.

Note: Fill in the blank with your class's grade. For example, *The first grade class had a farm.*
Additional verses: Substitute other animal names to continue the song. Replace the bolded words with
the sound the animal makes, substituting the first sound with the first sound in the name of the animal.
For example, *And on that farm we had a **duck**. E-I-E-I-O. With a **dack dack** here, and a **dack dack** there.*

Spring Phonemic Awareness Songs & Rhymes © 1998 Creative Teaching Press

♫ Silly Farm Song ♫

(sing to the tune of "The Wheels on the Bus")

The **rooster** on the farm says, "Cock-a-doodle-doo.

Rock-a-**r**oodle-**r**oo. **R**ock-a-**r**oodle-**r**oo."

The **rooster** on the farm says,

"Cock-a-doodle-doo,"

Down on the silly farm.

The **donkey** on the farm says, "Hee-haw.

Dee-**d**aw. **D**ee-**d**aw."

The **donkey** on the farm says,

"Hee-haw,"

Down on the silly farm.

The **sheep** on the farm says, "Baa, baa, baa.

Shaa, **sh**aa, **sh**aa. **Sh**aa, **sh**aa, **sh**aa."

The **sheep** on the farm says,

"Baa, baa, baa,"

Down on the silly farm.

Additional verses: Substitute other animal names to continue the song. Replace bolded words with the sound the animal makes, substituting the first sound with the first sound in the animal's name.

Little Red Hen

(sing to the tune of "Someone's in the Kitchen with Dinah")

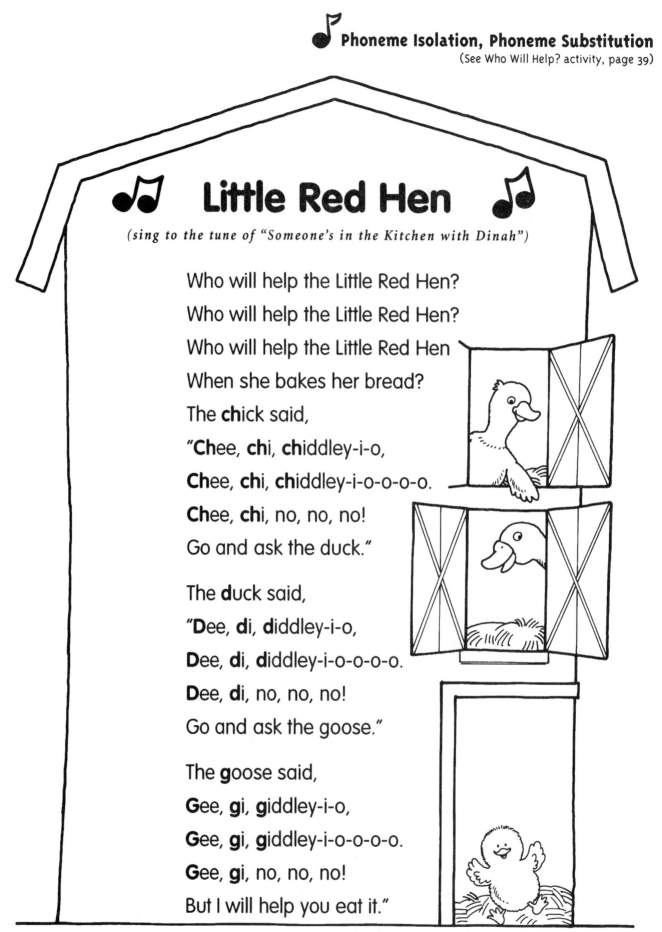

Who will help the Little Red Hen?

Who will help the Little Red Hen?

Who will help the Little Red Hen

When she bakes her bread?

The **ch**ick said,

"**Ch**ee, **ch**i, **ch**iddley-i-o,

Chee, **ch**i, **ch**iddley-i-o-o-o-o.

Chee, **ch**i, no, no, no!

Go and ask the duck."

The **d**uck said,

"**D**ee, **d**i, **d**iddley-i-o,

Dee, **d**i, **d**iddley-i-o-o-o-o.

Dee, **d**i, no, no, no!

Go and ask the goose."

The **g**oose said,

Gee, **g**i, **g**iddley-i-o,

Gee, **g**i, **g**iddley-i-o-o-o-o.

Gee, **g**i, no, no, no!

But I will help you eat it."

♫ It's Morning on the Farm ♫

(sing to the tune of "The Farmer in the Dell")

It's morning on the farm.
It's morning on the farm.
Hi-ho the derry-o,
It's morning on the farm.

I think I see a **c**ow.
I think I see a **c**ow.
Ki-**k**o the **k**erry-o,
I think I see a **c**ow.

Now I see a **p**ig.
Now I see a **p**ig.
Pi-**p**o the **p**erry-o,
Now I see a **p**ig.

Oh, is that a **d**uck?
Oh, is that a **d**uck?
Di-**d**o the **d**erry-o,
Oh, is that a **d**uck?

I think it's time to **g**o.
I think it's time to **g**o.
Gi-**g**o the **g**erry-o,
I think it's time to **g**o.
Good-bye!

♫ Down on the Farm

(sing to the tune of "Old MacDonald Had a Farm")

Danny and **David** had a farm. E-I-E-I-O.

And on that farm there was a **duck. D**e-**di**-**de**-**di**-**d**o.

With a **/d/ /d/** here,

And a **/d/ /d/** there.

Here a **/d/**. There a **/d/**.

Everywhere a **/d/ /d/**.

Danny and **David** had a farm. **D**e-**di**-**de**-**di**-**d**o.

Paige and **Paul** had a farm. E-I-E-I-O.

And on that farm there was a **pig. P**e-**pi**-**pe**-**pi**-**p**o.

With a **/p/ /p/** here,

And a **/p/ /p/** there.

Here a **/p/**. There a **/p/**.

Everywhere a **/p/ /p/**.

Paige and **Paul** had a farm. **P**e-**pi**-**pe**-**pi**-**p**o.

Additional verses: Replace names with student names that begin with the same sound. Then, replace the animal name with an animal that begins with the same sound. Have students substitute the first sound for the beginning sound in the animal's name. For example, *Chelsea* and *Chase* had a farm. *E-I-E-I-O. And on that farm there was a* **chick.** *Che-chi-che-chi-cho.*

Spring Phonemic Awareness Songs & Rhymes © 1998 Creative Teaching Press

 # Guess My Animal

(sing to the tune of "The Muffin Man")

Can you guess my animal,
My animal, my animal?
Can you guess my animal?
It lives on the farm.

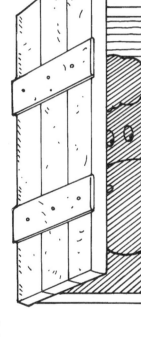

My animal says **/m/ /oo/,**
/m/ /oo/, /m/ /oo/.
My animal says **moo.**
My animal is a **cow.**

My animal says **/oi/ /n/ /k/,**
/oi/ /n/ /k/, /oi/ /n/ /k/.
My animal says **oink.**
My animal is a **pig.**

My animal says **/b/ /a/,**
/b/ /a/, /b/ /a/.
My animal says **baa.**
My animal is a **sheep.**

Additional verses: Replace the bolded words and phonemes with other animals and the sounds they make. Separate the sounds and have students blend them to discover the animal. For example, *My animal says* */p/ /ee/ /p/, /p/ /ee/ /p/, /p/ /ee/ /p/. My animal says* **peep.** *My animal is a* **chick.**

♫ **Big Red Barn** ♫

(sing to the tune of "Where, Oh, Where Has My Little Dog Gone?")

I wonder what's in the big red barn.

I wonder what's in it for me.

It starts with **/k/,**

And it rhymes with **now.**

Oh, what do you think it could be?

It starts with **/ch/,**

And it rhymes with **lick.**

Oh, what do you think it could be?

It starts with **/p/,**

And it rhymes with **wig.**

Oh, what do you think it could be?

Additional verses: Replace the bolded phonemes and words to continue the song. For example, *It starts with /g/, and it rhymes with **moose.** Oh, what do you think it could be?*

The Talking Farm Animals

(sing to the tune of "Looby Loo")

The animals like to talk
In a special way.
The animals like to talk.
What does the **pig** say?

Here we go **p**ooby **p**oo,
Here we go **p**ooby **p**ay,
Here we go **p**ooby **p**oo.
Now what would the little **chick** say?

Here we go **ch**ooby **ch**oo,
Here we go **ch**ooby **ch**ay,
Here we go **ch**ooby **ch**oo.
Now what would the big **goat** say?

Here we go **g**ooby **g**oo,
Here we go **g**ooby **g**ay,
Here we go **g**ooby **g**oo.
I could sing this song all day.

Additional verses: Replace bolded animal names and the bolded sounds to continue the song.

Farm Animals Change Their Tune

(sing to the tune of "Deck the Halls")

Here's a song that changes first sounds.

La la la la la, la la la la.

Let's try singing with the **/k/** sound.

Ka **k**a **k**a **k**a **k**a, **k**a **k**a **k**a **k**a.

Colt and **calf** begin with the **/k/** sound.

Ka **k**a **k**a, **k**a **k**a **k**a, **k**a **k**a **k**a.

Now let's change it back to the /l/ sound.

La la la la la, la la la la!

Here's a song that changes last sounds.

La la la la la, la la la la.

Let's try singing with the **/ee/** sound.

Lee lee lee lee lee, lee lee lee lee.

Puppy and **kitty** end with the **/ee/** sound.

Lee lee lee, lee lee lee, lee lee lee.

Now let's change it back to the /a/ sound.

La la la la la, la la la la!

Note: Sing the song with beginning or ending sound changes many times before attempting to change beginning and ending sounds in the same session.
Additional verses: Replace the bolded sounds and words to continue the song. For example, *Let's try singing with the /r/ sound. Ra ra ra ra ra, ra ra ra ra. Rooster and rabbit begin with the /r/ sound.*

♫ Farm Animals ♫
(sing to the tune of "Six Little Ducks")

I see some animals little and big,

A rooster, a turkey, and a pig.

But the one on the farm

That rhymes with **now**

Is my favorite.

It's the **cow.**

Additional verses: Replace the bolded words to continue the song. For example, *But the one on the farm that rhymes with **wig** is my favorite. It's the **pig.***

♫ The Little Chick ♫

(sing to the tune of "Willoughby, Wallaby, Woo")

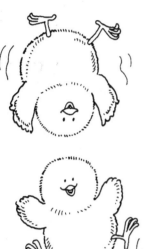

Chickity, chackity, chee,
A chick flew over me.
Chickity, chackity, choo,
The chick flew over you.

Chickity, chackity, ch**ooke,**
The chick flew over **Brooke,**
Chickity, chackity, ch**asey,**
The chick flew over **Casey.**

Additional verses: Replace the bolded names to continue the song. Substitute the initial sound with /ch/. For example, *Chickity, chackity, cheff, the chick flew over Jeff.*

Spring Phonemic Awareness Songs & Rhymes © 1998 Creative Teaching Press

Listen to the Farm Sounds

(sing to the tune of "Who's Afraid of the Big, Bad Wolf?")

What's the first sound you hear in **horse,**

You hear in **hay,** you hear in **hen?**

The first sound that we hear

Is **/h/ /h/ /h/ /h/ /h/.**

What's the last sound you hear in **barn,**

You hear in **pen,** you hear in **chicken?**

The last sound that we hear

Is **/n/ /n/ /n/ /n/ /n/.**

Note: Pause for students to sing the last line.
Additional verses: Replace the bolded words with other farm-related words with the same beginning or ending sound to continue the song.

Silly Sounds from the Farm

Phoneme Substitution

Materials

- Barn reproducible (page 87)
- crayons or markers
- scissors
- glue
- construction paper
- speech bubbles

Give each student a copy of the Barn reproducible to decorate and cut out. Have students cut on the dotted lines and fold the barn doors open. Invite students to glue their barn to construction paper, leaving the doors folded open. Have each student illustrate a different farm animal, cut it out, and glue it behind the barn doors so the doors open to reveal the animal. Have students complete on their paper the frame *The _____ in the barn says. . . .* Invite students to create speech bubbles for their animal and write the sound the animal makes, substituting the initial sound with the initial sound of the animal's name. Have students glue their speech bubbles inside the doors. For example, *The rooster in the barn says, "Rock-a-roodle-roo."*

(Use with "On Our Farm," page 26)

Farm Animal Lotto

Sound Matching, Phoneme Isolation

Materials

- Farm Animals reproducible (page 88)
- manipulatives (beans or corn kernels)

Distribute copies of the Farm Animals reproducible. Give each student a handful of farm-related manipulatives such as beans or corn kernels to be used as markers. Give clues to students such as *Place a marker on the animal whose name begins with /k/ and ends with /t/.* Watch students as they place a marker on the correct animal.

(Use with "Silly Farm Song," page 27)

Who Will Help?

Phoneme Isolation, Phoneme Substitution

Give one animal from the Animals reproducible to each student. Have students color, cut out, and glue their animal to a construction-paper strip to make a headband. Staple the strips to fit each student's head. Have students sit in a circle while wearing their headband. Have the "hens" sit in the center of the circle and sing "Little Red Hen" while the other students pass around a loaf of bread. The last word of the song will be the name of the animal on the headband of the student left holding the bread. For example, students sing *Go and ask the **goose*** if the student holding the bread is wearing the goose

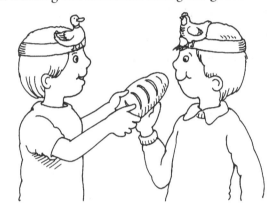

headband. All students wearing a goose headband take the place of the hens in the center of the circle and the "goose" verse is sung while the bread is passed again. Continue until all students have sat in the center.

(Use with "Little Red Hen," page 28)

Materials

- "Little Red Hen" song (page 28)

- Animals reproducible (page 89)

- crayons or markers

- scissors

- glue

- construction-paper strips

- stapler

- bread loaf

ABCs Farm Class Book

Sound Matching

After singing each stanza of "It's Morning on the Farm," ask the class to think of other things on the farm that start with the same sound and draw them on drawing paper. For example, after singing *Di-do the derry-o, oh, is that a duck?*

students could draw a dog, daisy, door on a barn, or dump truck. Have students cut out the objects and glue them onto construction paper. Include one page for each letter of the alphabet and bind the pages together. Title the class book *ABCs on the Farm*.

(Use with "It's Morning on the Farm," page 29)

Materials

- "It's Morning on the Farm" song (page 29)

- drawing paper

- crayons or markers

- scissors

- glue

- construction paper

Our Farm

Sound Matching, Phoneme Isolation, Phoneme Addition

- "Down on the Farm" song (page 30)

- index cards

- student photos

- glue

- chart paper

- pointers

Write each child's name on an index card and glue the student's photo to the card. Make a word wall on chart paper, including a column for each letter of the alphabet. Place the photo name cards under the appropriate letter. For columns that have fewer than two names, brainstorm with the class names that begin with those letters or sounds, write the names on blank index cards, and add them to the word wall. Write on an index card the name of an animal that begins with each sound and place it on the word wall. Invite students to use pointers while singing "Down on the Farm."

(Use with "Down on the Farm," page 30)

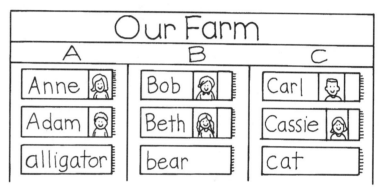

Pig Pen

Phoneme Blending, Phoneme Segmentation

Materials

- none

This game is a variation of Duck, Duck, Goose. Have students sit in a circle. Choose one student to be the "farmer." Have the farmer tap the head of each student as he or she says each sound in a farm animal's name. For example, the farmer says /p/ /i/ /g/ /p/ /i/ /g/ /p/ /i/ /g/ Pig! The last student tapped then chases the farmer around the circle. If the farmer is tagged, he or she must sit in the "pig pen." The new farmer continues the game with another animal's name.

(Use with "Guess My Animal," page 31)

Barnyard Box

Rhyming, Phoneme Substitution

In advance, make a copy of the Barn reproducible, color it red, and glue it to a cereal box. Hide small plastic farm animals in the box. Sing "Big Red Barn" with your students. After each stanza, invite a student to find the farm animal in the "barn" that completes the rhyme.

(Use with "Big Red Barn," page 32)

Materials

- "Big Red Barn" song (page 32)

- Barn reproducible (page 87)

- red crayons or markers

- cereal box

- glue

- small plastic farm animals

Animal Visors

Sound Matching, Phoneme Substitution

Invite students to draw on construction paper an upside-down rainbow shape to make a visor. Have students cut it out and decorate it like a farm animal.

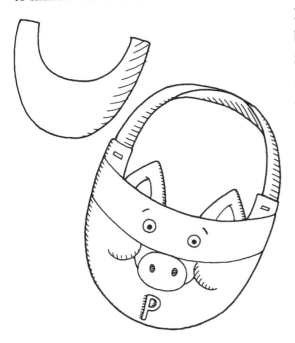

Have students write the animal's beginning sound on the visor. Staple elastic to each side and invite students to wear their visor as they role-play and sing "The Talking Farm Animals." As an extension, invite students to name foods that start with the same sound as their animal's name. For example, *My pig eats potatoes, peanuts, and popcorn.*

(Use with "The Talking Farm Animals," page 33)

Materials

- "The Talking Farm Animals" song (page 33)

- construction paper

- crayons or markers

- scissors

- stapler

- elastic

Farming for Animals
Sound Matching, Phoneme Isolation, Phoneme Substitution

Materials

- "Farm Animals Change Their Tune" song (page 34)

- plastic farm animals

Invite a student to choose a plastic farm animal and say the first sound of the animal's name. Brainstorm with the class other items or animals found on a farm that begin with that sound and list them on the board. Invite students to sing "Farm Animals Change Their Tune," using the chosen sound and listed words to change the tune. For example, if a student chooses a horse, the class sings *Let's try singing with the /h/ sound. Ha ha ha ha ha, ha ha ha ha. Horse and hay begin with the /h/ sound.* Invite another student to choose an animal to continue the game. For a greater challenge, invite students to isolate the ending sound of the animal's name.

(Use with "Farm Animals Change Their Tune," page 34)

b	c	d
barn barley bull banjo	cat crops corn	duck dog dirt

Rhyme It!
Rhyming

Materials

- "Farm Animals" song (page 35)

- Farm Animals reproducible (page 88)

- scissors

- box or bag

Cut apart the pictures from the Farm Animals reproducible and place them in a box or bag. Call a volunteer to select a picture. The student, with help from the class if necessary, thinks of a rhyming word for that animal. Invite the class to then sing "Farm Animals" using the student's rhyme. Continue playing with another volunteer.

(Use with "Farm Animals," page 35)

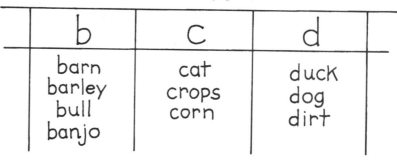

Three Cheers for Our Chick
Phoneme Substitution

Have children sit in a close circle. Explain that the "Little Chick" loves to fly, but is young and does not like to fly high (establishing the rules for tossing the chick). While singing "The Little Chick," invite students to "fly" the chick to the student whose name is sung next. For example, while students sing *Chickity, chackity, chilly,* a student tosses the chick to Billy. Then Billy tosses it to the next student whose name is sung.

(Use with "The Little Chick," page 36)

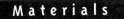

Chickity, chackity, chilly...

Sound Scavenger Hunt
Sound Matching

In advance, ask office staff or nearby teachers if students may visit to collect items for their sound scavenger hunt. Children will ask for an item that begins with the same sound as the sound or blend on their sack. To prepare the sacks, glue a photocopy of the Barn reproducible to four paper grocery sacks and

write a different sound or blend on each barn. Divide the class into four groups and give each group a sack. Invite students to visit the selected rooms. When the groups return, have them give clues as to what they found. (Be sure students return the collected items.)

(Use with "Listen to the Farm Sounds," page 37)

Materials

- Barn reproducible (page 87)

- 4 paper grocery sacks

- glue

Come Swim with Me

(sing to the tune of "Down by the Bay")

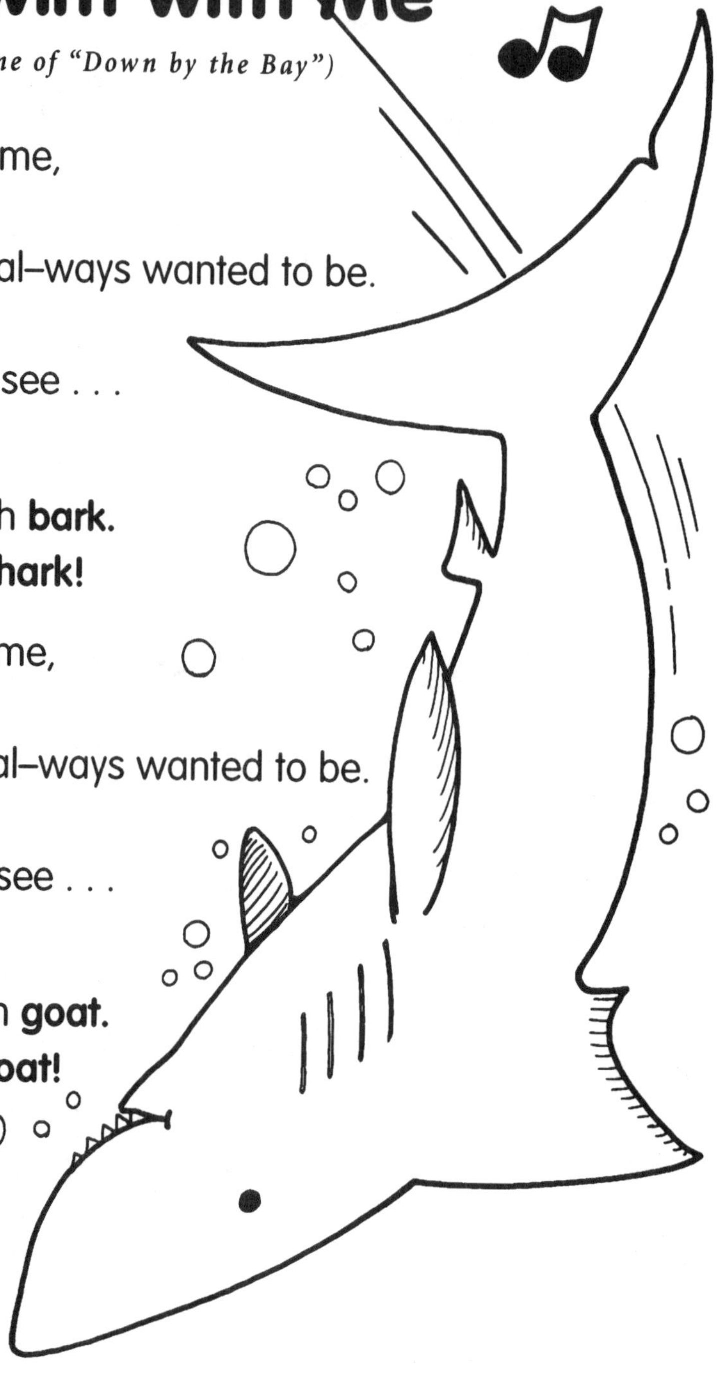

Come swim with me,
Deep in the sea.
That's where I've al–ways wanted to be.
And when we go
Guess what we'll see . . .

It starts with **/sh/**
And it rhymes with **bark.**
We might see a **shark!**

Come swim with me,
Deep in the sea.
That's where I've al–ways wanted to be.
And when we go
Guess what we'll see . . .

It starts with **/b/**
And it rhymes with **goat.**
We might see a **boat!**

Additional verses: Replace the bolded phonemes and words with other items found in the sea to continue the song. For example, *It starts with /sh/ and it rhymes with bell. We might see a shell!*

Spring Phonemic Awareness Songs & Rhymes © 1998 Creative Teaching Press

Beach Riddles

(sing to the tune of "The Wheels on the Bus")

I live in the ocean and I like to crawl,

I like to crawl, I like to crawl.

I live in the ocean and I like to crawl.

My name rhymes with **lab**.

I live in the ocean and I like to swim,

I like to swim, I like to swim.

I live in the ocean and I like to swim.

My name rhymes with **wish**.

I live in the ocean and I like to bite,

I like to bite, I like to bite.

I live in the ocean and I like to bite.

My name rhymes with **bark**.

♫ Down by the Ocean ♫

(sing to the tune of "You Are My Sunshine")

Down by the ocean,
Down by the sea,
I saw a **lobster**
Crawl right by me.
I said, "Hey, **lobster**,
What's your first sound?
Is it **/p/, /l/,** or **/t/?"**

Down by the ocean,
Down by the sea,
I saw a big **fish**
Swim right by me.
I said, "Hey, **fish**,
What's your first sound?
Is it **/f/, /a/,** or **/z/?"**

Down by the ocean,
Down by the sea,
I saw a **jellyfish**
Float right by me.
I said, "Hey, **jellyfish**,
What's your first sound?
Is it **/b/, /d/,** or **/j/?"**

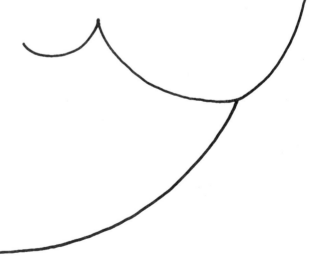

What Lives in the Sea?

(sing to the tune of "Do Your Ears Hang Low?")

Let's all sing an ocean song,

Everyone can sing along.

When you listen with your ear,

Many sounds you will hear.

I will say a word slow

And you say it when you know . . .

What lives in the sea?

/f/ /i/ /sh/

/ee/ /l/

/shr/ /i/ /m/ /p/

/wh/ /a/ /l/

Note: Have students blend the phonemes and say each word.

Spring Phonemic Awareness Songs & Rhymes © 1998 Creative Teaching Press

♫ Diving Down ♫

(Sing to the tune of "My Bonnie Lies over the Ocean")

I'm diving down deep in the ocean.
I'm diving down deep in the sea.
I'm diving down deep in the ocean.
Oh, what do you think I will see?

F–ish, f–ish,

I hope to see **fish** today, today.

F–ish, f–ish,

What else do you think I will see?

C–oral, c–oral,

I hope to see **coral** today, today.

C–oral, c–oral,

What else do you think I will see?

Note: Invite volunteers to choose an item and separate the onset and
rime. Then have the class blend the word.
Additional verses: Replace bolded words to continue the song. For
example, *Shr—imp, shr—imp, I hope to see* **shrimp** *today, today.*

♫ Fishing for a Rhyme ♫♫

(sing to the tune of "A-Hunting We Will Go")

A-fishing we will go.

A-fishing we will go.

We'll catch a **whale**

And put it in a **pail**

And then we'll let it go.

A-fishing we will go.

A-fishing we will go.

We'll catch a **shark**

And put it in the **dark**

And then we'll let it go.

A-fishing we will go.

A-fishing we will go.

We'll catch a **fish**

And put it on a **dish**

And then we'll let it go.

Additional verses: Replace bolded rhyming words to continue the song. For example,
*We'll catch a **seal** and give it a **meal*** or *We'll catch a **shell** and teach it to **spell**.*

♫ In My Bucket ♫

(sing to the tune of "Clementine")

In my bucket, in my bucket

That I carry to the beach,

I put a **starfish** and a **seashell**

And a **sandwich** I can eat.

If I want to add some more things,

Tell me what else should I bring?

I can only carry items with the first sound **/s/**.

In my bucket, in my bucket

That I carry to the beach

I put a **penny** and a **peanut**

And a **pickle** I can eat.

If I want to add some more things,

Tell me what else should I bring?

I can only carry items with the first sound **/p/**.

Additional verses: Replace bolded words and phonemes to continue the song.
For example, *I put a **beach ball** and a **bikini** and a **banana** I can eat.*

Spring Phonemic Awareness Songs & Rhymes © 1998 Creative Teaching Press

Catch It!

(sing to the tune of "My Bonnie Lies over the Ocean")

A **sh–ark** lives down in the ocean.

A **sh–ark** lives down in the sea.

A **sh–ark** lives down in the ocean.

Oh, please catch a **shark** for me.

Sh–ark, sh–ark,

Oh, please catch a **shark** for me, for me.

Sh–ark, sh–ark,

Oh, please catch a **shark** for me.

A **cr–ab** lives down in the ocean.

A **cr–ab** lives down in the sea.

A **cr–ab** lives down in the ocean.

Oh, please catch a **crab** for me.

Cr–ab, cr–ab,

Oh, please catch a **crab** for me, for me.

Cr–ab, cr–ab,

Oh, please catch a **crab** for me.

Note: Have students segment the onset and rime during the second stanza.

Additional verses: Replace the bolded words with other ocean-dwelling animals to continue the song. For example, *A **st–arfish** lives down in the ocean.*

What Will We See?

Rhyming, Phoneme Substitution

(Use with "Come Swim with Me," page 44)

Materials

- "Come Swim with Me" song (page 44)
- Deep Sea Picture Cards (page 90)
- scissors
- tape or magnetic strips
- colored chalk or wipe-off markers
- glue
- die-cut alphabet letters
- craft sticks

In advance, photocopy the Deep Sea Picture Cards, cut them out, and place tape or magnetic strips on the back of each card. Draw an ocean background on the board. Glue alphabet letters to craft sticks and distribute them to students. Display the picture cards on the board, sing "Come Swim with Me" with your students, and have students stand when they are holding a craft stick with the beginning sound. When students make a rhyme, ask a volunteer to find the correct picture card and add it to the scene.

Who Am I?

Rhyming

Materials

- "Beach Riddles" song (page 45)
- sentence strips
- pocket chart
- construction paper
- crayons or markers

Write on sentence strips *I live in the ocean and I like to _____. My name rhymes with _____.* Place the sentence strips in a pocket chart. Sing "Beach Riddles" with your class. Then, divide the class into small groups and invite each group to fill in the blanks to create a new rhyme to add to the song. Distribute construction paper and invite students to draw the answer to their beach riddle and hold it up for the class.

(Use with "Beach Riddles," page 45)

Fishy Alphabet

Phoneme Isolation

Write each letter of the alphabet on a fish cutout and attach a paper clip or Velcro strip to each. Scatter the cutouts on a large blue butcher-paper "ocean." Tie yarn to a yardstick or dowel and attach a magnet or Velcro strip to the end. Sing "Down by the Ocean" with your class and invite students to "fish" for the correct letter.

(Use with "Down by the Ocean," page 46)

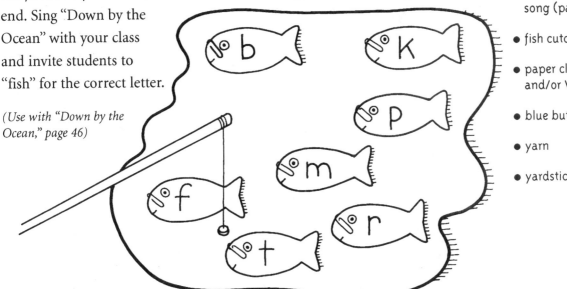

Materials

- "Down by the Ocean" song (page 46)
- fish cutouts
- paper clips, magnets and/or Velcro strips
- blue butcher paper
- yarn
- yardstick or dowel

Pass the Pail

Syllable Counting, Phoneme Blending, Phoneme Segmentation

Have students sit in a circle. Fill a bucket with items related to the beach and pass it around the circle. Invite a volunteer to secretly choose an item from the bucket. Have that child segment the sounds of the item (or split the onset and rime) for the class to blend. Then, ask the volunteer to hold up the item. Next, have the class clap the syllables in the word. As an extension, invite students to sort the items into groups based on the number of syllables.

(Use with "What Lives in the Sea?" page 47)

Materials

- beach bucket
- beach-related items and creatures

Sounds of the Sea
Phoneme Blending, Phoneme Counting, Phoneme Segmentation

Materials

- "Diving Down" song (page 48)
- items found in the sea (plastic fish or shark, seaweed, shell, toy boat, old shoe)
- small plastic pool

Place ocean-related objects in a small plastic pool. While the class sings "Diving Down," invite a "scuba diver" to blend the sounds of and locate an object or animal in the pool. For a greater challenge, hold up an item from the pool and have the class separate the sounds in the name. Ask students to clap for each sound and count how many sounds they hear in the word.

(Use with "Diving Down," page 48)

Catch a Rhyme
Rhyming

Materials

- "Fishing for a Rhyme" song (page 49)
- Deep Sea Picture Cards (page 90)
- string
- magnet
- yardstick or dowel
- index cards
- crayons or markers
- paper clips
- fishbowl

In advance, prepare a "rod" by attaching string and a magnet to a yardstick or dowel. Give each student a photocopy of the Deep Sea Picture Cards. Invite students to draw on index cards pictures of items that rhyme with the picture cards and have them attach a paper clip to each card. Collect in a fishbowl the students' pictures and invite a volunteer to go "fish." Invite the student to find the rhyming match and create a rhyming phrase for "Fishing for a Rhyme." Continue fishing until all animals are "caught."

(Use with "Fishing for a Rhyme," page 49)

Picture Pail
Sound Matching

Photocopy the Beach Picture Cards and distribute one set to each student. Have students color them and cut them out. Ask students to draw on index cards other items and foods that begin with the same sound as one or two of the picture cards. Have students sit in a circle, and place a beach bucket in the middle of the circle. As you sing "In My Bucket," ask a student to place a picture card in the bucket. Invite others to add items they drew that begin with the same sound, or pass the bucket for students to orally share what they would add that begins with the same sound.

(Use with "In My Bucket," page 50)

Materials

- "In My Bucket" song (page 50)
- Beach Picture Cards (page 91)
- crayons or markers
- scissors
- index cards
- beach bucket

Match It!
Syllable Splitting, Phoneme Blending

Write on sentence strips animal names that live in the ocean and draw or glue on each strip a picture of the animal. Cut apart each sentence strip so the onset and rime (and the picture) are on two different pieces. Mix up all the cut sentence strips and place them in a pocket chart. Sing "Catch It!" with students and invite them to match the onset with the rime as they blend the word.

(Use with "Catch It!" page 51)

Materials

- "Catch It!" song (page 51)
- sentence strips
- crayons or animal pictures and glue
- scissors
- pocket chart

♫ Playing with the Animals

(sing to the tune of "This Old Man")

In the spring,

We see the sun

And lots of animals having fun.

We see a chick, a pony, a bunny, and a ram.

We can even see a baby lamb.

Guess what animal I can see.

Guess what animal is playing with me.

It begins with **/k/**

And ends with **/itten/.**

Yes, I'm playing with a baby **kitten.**

Guess what animal I can see.

Guess what animal is playing with me.

It begins with **/b/**

And ends with **/unny/.**

Yes, I'm playing with a baby **bunny.**

Additional verses: Replace the bolded sounds and words to continue the song. For example, *It begins with **/k/** and ends with **/olt/**. Yes, I'm playing with a baby **colt**.*

Spring Phonemic Awareness Songs & Rhymes © 1998 Creative Teaching Press

I'm a Baby Animal

(sing to the tune of "Little White Duck")

I'm a baby animal.

My name begins with **/ch/**.

I'm a baby animal.

My name begins with **/ch/**.

It has three sounds.

What do you think I am?

A **chick,** a **duck,** or a **baby lamb?**

I'm a baby animal.

My name begins with **/ch/**.

Yes, I'm a **chick!**

Additional verses: Replace the bolded phonemes and words to continue the song. For example, *I'm a baby animal. My name begins with **/p/**. It has three sounds. What do you think I am? A **calf,** a **lamb,** or a **playful pup?***

I Wish I Were an Animal
(sing to the tune of "Oscar Mayer Weiner")

Oh, I wish I were a woolly little /l/ /a/ /m/.

That is what I'd really like to be.

For if I were a woolly little **lamb,**

Then everyone would want to play with me!

Oh, I wish I were a fuzzy little /ch/ /i/ /k/.

That is what I'd really like to be.

For if I were a fuzzy little **chick,**

Then everyone would want to play with me!

Oh, I wish I were a soft little /k/ /i/ /t/ /e/ /n/.

That is what I'd really like to be.

For if I were a soft little **kitten,**

Then everyone would want to play with me!

Oh, I wish I were a fluffy little /d/ /u/ /k/.

That is what I'd really like to be.

For if I were a fluffy little **duck,**

Then everyone would want to play with me!

Additional verses: Replace the bolded phonemes and words to continue the song. For example, *Oh, I wish I were a cute little /p/ /u/ /p/ /ee/.* Pause for students to blend the sounds.

Spring Phonemic Awareness Songs & Rhymes © 1998 Creative Teaching Press

♫ Playful Animals ♫

(sing to the tune of "Mary Had a Little Lamb")

We can see a little **white duck.**

/d/ /u/ /k/, /d/ /u/ /k/.

We can see a little **white duck.**

He is playing with a **chick.**

We can see a little **yellow chick.**

/ch/ /i/ /k/, /ch/ /i/ /k/.

We can see a little **yellow chick.**

She is playing with a **goat.**

We can see a little **brown goat.**

/g/ /oa/ /t/, /g/ /oa/ /t/.

We can see a little **brown goat.**

He is playing with a **pig.**

Note: Have students sing the second line of each stanza by themselves.
Additional verses: Replace bolded words and phonemes to continue the song. For example,
*We can see a little **pink pig.** /p/ /i/ /g/, /p/ /i/ /g/.*

♫ The Silly Animals

(sing to the tune of "Zip-a-Dee-Doo-Dah")

Zip-a-dee-doo-dah, zip-a-dee-ay,
My, oh my, what a silly day.
Zip-a-dee-doo-dah, zip-a-dee-ay,
Geese sing this song in a silly way!

Gip-a-**g**ee-**g**oo-**g**ah, **g**ip-a-**g**ee-ay
My, oh my, what a silly day.
Gip-a-**g**ee-**g**oo-**g**ah, **g**ip-a-**g**ee-ay,
Pigs sing this song in a silly way!

Pip-a-**p**ee-**p**oo-**p**ah, **p**ip-a-**p**ee-ay
My, oh my, what a silly day.
Pip-a-**p**ee-**p**oo-**p**ah, **p**ip-a-**p**ee-ay,
Horses sing this song in a silly way!

Hip-a-**h**ee-**h**oo-**h**ah, **h**ip-a-**h**ee-ay
My, oh my, what a silly day.
Hip-a-**h**ee-**h**oo-**h**ah, **h**ip-a-**h**ee-ay,
Animals sing this song in a silly way!

Additional verses: Replace bolded words to continue the song. For example, ***Dogs*** *sing this song in a silly way!* Dip-a-*dee-doo-dah, dip-a-dee-ay.*

♫ What's in the Egg? ♫

(sing to the tune of "Who's Afraid of the Big, Bad Wolf?")

What comes out of the little brown egg,
The little brown egg, the little brown egg?
What comes out of the little brown egg
That will rhyme with **rake?**

What comes out of the little yellow egg,
The little yellow egg, the little yellow egg?
What comes out of the little yellow egg
That will rhyme with **stick?**

What comes out of the little blue egg,
The little blue egg, the little blue egg?
What comes out of the little blue egg
That will rhyme with **rug?**

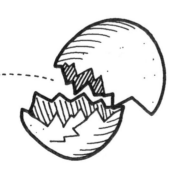

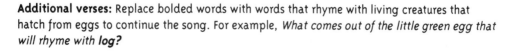

Additional verses: Replace bolded words with words that rhyme with living creatures that hatch from eggs to continue the song. For example, *What comes out of the little green egg that will rhyme with **log?***

Find the Baby Animals

Phoneme Blending

Materials

- "Playing with the Animals" song (page 56)

- Baby Animal Picture Cards (page 92)

- sentence strips

- pocket chart

In advance, write on sentence strips the onset and rime to each animal from the Baby Animal Picture Cards and place them randomly in the pocket chart with the picture cards. After singing "Playing with the Animals," show a picture to the class and have students locate the matching onset and rime and place them next to the picture.

(Use with "Playing with the Animals," page 56)

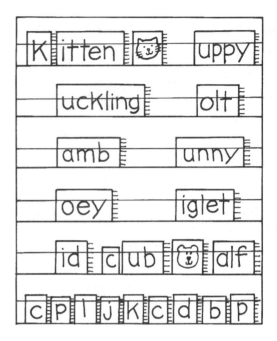

Baby Sounds

Phoneme Isolation, Phoneme Counting

Materials

- "I'm a Baby Animal" song (page 57)

- Baby Animal Picture Cards (page 92)

- pocket chart

Photocopy the Baby Animal Picture Cards and cut them out. Sing "I'm a Baby Animal." For each set of three animals, display those picture cards in a pocket chart. While singing, the children can see their choices clearly and refer to them if they need more help. Remind students to listen to how many sounds each baby animal has in its name. Then, have a child hold up the correct picture and restate how many sounds are in the word. As an extension, have students locate the animal according to its ending sound.

(Use with "I'm a Baby Animal," page 57)

Rolling in the Hay

Phoneme Counting, Phoneme Segmentation

Photocopy the Baby Animal Picture Cards and cut them out. Tape a picture card to each side of the half-pint milk cartons to create "dice." Divide the class into two groups. Have each group roll a die and segment the name of the pictured animal. Ask each student who rolls the die to count how many sounds were in the word.

(Use with "I Wish I Were an Animal," page 58)

(Use with "I Wish I Were an Animal," page 58)

Materials

- Baby Animal Picture Cards (page 92)
- scissors
- tape
- 2 half-pint milk cartons

Name That Animal

Phoneme Counting, Phoneme Segmentation

Have students set their chairs in a circle facing outward. Reproduce the Baby Animal Picture Cards and the Farm Animals reproducible and cut them out. Place a picture card on each chair. (Some chairs can be without cards.) While music is playing, have students walk around the chairs. When the music stops, have students sit down in the closest chair and look at their picture card (if they have one). Select a few students to name their card and clap the sounds. Ask for a volunteer to name a word that rhymes with his or her animal. Continue the game so several students segment words.

(Use with "Playful Animals," page 59)

(Use with "Playful Animals," page 59)

Materials

- "Playful Animals" song (page 59)
- Farm Animals reproducible (page 88)
- Baby Animal Picture Cards (page 92)
- chairs
- music

Animal Antics

Phoneme Substitution

Materials

● "The Silly Animals" song (page 60)

Divide the class into animal teams. Ask the first team to choose an animal and sing the first stanza of "The Silly Animals," including the name of their animal in the last verse. The second team sings the next stanza, substituting the first sound of the animal the first team sang and ending their verse with another animal. This continues until all teams have played.

(Use with "The Silly Animals," page 60)

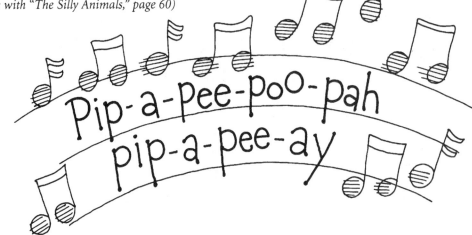

Look What's Hatching

Rhyming

Materials

● construction paper

● scissors

● gold brads

● crayons or markers

● glue

● butcher paper

Have each child cut out a large egg shape from construction paper and cut it zigzagged across the middle to resemble a cracked egg. Have students attach a brad to one end so the egg can "crack" open. Invite each student to draw an animal that hatches from an egg (e.g., birds, reptiles, and insects), cut it out, and glue it to a construction-paper sheet. Have students place their egg over the animal and poke the brad through the construction paper so the animal can peek through the egg's opening. Have students complete on the construction-paper sheet the sentence frame *What will hatch from the little _____ egg that will rhyme with _____?* Display the eggs in a huge butcher-paper "nest" on a bulletin board titled *Look What's Hatching in Room _____.*

What will hatch from the little white egg that will rhyme with brick?

(Use with "What's in the Egg?" page 61)

♫ Coloring Eggs

(sing to the tune of "Six Little Ducks")

Coloring eggs is what I like to do.

I like them green and yellow, too.

But the one little egg that rhymes with **ink**

Is my favorite color.

It's the color **pink.**

Additional verses: Replace the bolded words with other colors and rhymes to continue the song.
For example, *But the one little egg that rhymes with **bed** is my favorite color. It's the color **red.***

♪ Packing for a Picnic ♪

(sing to the tune of "Three Blind Mice")

Packing for a picnic,

Packing for a picnic.

What will we bring?

What will we bring?

Carly will bring **carrots**.

Jack will bring **jelly**.

Pat will bring **pizza**.

And **Frankie** will bring **french fries**.

Note: Say a name and have that student name a food item that begins with the same sound.

Additional verses: Replace the bolded names and foods with student names and food items that begin with the same sound to continue the song. For example, *Susie will bring **celery**.*

Spring Phonemic Awareness Songs & Rhymes © 1998 Creative Teaching Press

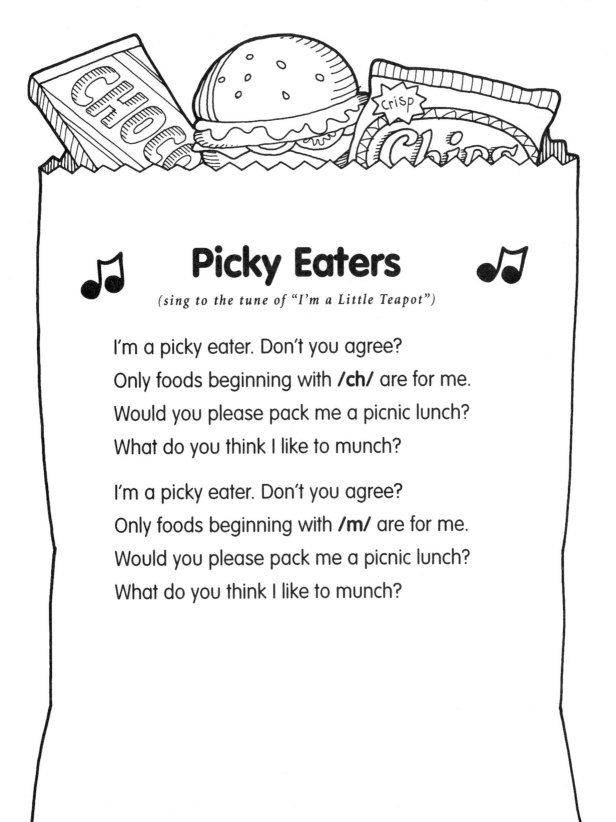

Picky Eaters

(sing to the tune of "I'm a Little Teapot")

I'm a picky eater. Don't you agree?

Only foods beginning with **/ch/** are for me.

Would you please pack me a picnic lunch?

What do you think I like to munch?

I'm a picky eater. Don't you agree?

Only foods beginning with **/m/** are for me.

Would you please pack me a picnic lunch?

What do you think I like to munch?

Note: Have students respond after each stanza. For example,
chips, chili, cheeseburgers or *meatballs, mangoes, melons.*
Additional verses: Replace bolded sounds to continue the song.

Picnic Lunch

(sing to the tune of "Yankee Doodle")

I'm going to pack a picnic lunch.

Can you guess what's in it?

It starts with **sand** and ends with **wich.**

A **sandwich.** I will eat it.

I'm going to pack a picnic lunch.

Can you guess what's in it?

It starts with **lemon** and ends with **ade.**

Lemonade. I will drink it.

I'm going to pack a picnic lunch.

Can you guess what's in it?

It starts with **ch** and ends with **ips.**

Some **chips.** I will eat them.

I'm going to pack a picnic lunch.

Can you guess what's in it?

It starts with **cook** and ends with **ies.**

Some **cookies.** I will eat them.

Additional verses: Replace the bolded words to continue the song. For example,
*It starts with **water** and ends with **melon.** A **watermelon.** I will eat it.*

Spring Phonemic Awareness Songs & Rhymes © 1998 Creative Teaching Press

♫ The Hungry Thing ♫ Goes on a Picnic

(sing to the tune of "The Beverly Hillbillies")

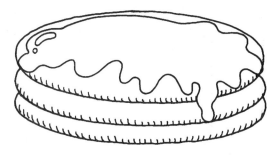

I met the Hungry Thing
And he wanted some food.
I listened very carefully
And finally understood.
When he asked for a **shookie,**
What he wanted was a **cookie.**
And now I'll give him what he really wants to eat.

When he asks for a **shancake,**
I know he wants a **pancake.**
When he asks for a **shacker,**
I know he wants a **cracker.**
When he asks for a **shupcake,**
I know he wants a **cupcake.**
Now I'll end my song, you see,
Because he's very hungry!

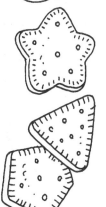

Additional verses: Replace bolded words and add a new beginning sound to the food items to continue the song. For example, *When he asks for a **chandwich**, I know he wants a **sandwich**.*

Little Green Frog

(sing to the tune of "Little White Duck")

I'm a little green frog,

Sitting in the water.

A little green frog,

Doing what I oughta.

A little black **/b/ /u/ /g/** came flying by.

I ate it up and I said, "Good-bye."

I'm a little green frog, sitting in the water.

Bye, bye, **bug!**

I'm a little green frog.

Sitting in the water.

A little green frog,

Doing what I oughta.

A little blue **/m/ /o/ /th/** came flying by.

I ate it up and I said, "Good-bye."

I'm a little green frog, sitting in the water.

Bye, bye, **moth!**

Additional verses: Replace bolded phonemes to continue the song. For example, *A little yellow /b/ /ee/ came flying by.*

🎵 Jelly Beans 🎵

(sing to the tune of "Ten Little Indians")

Pick up a jelly bean and put it in my mouth,

Pick up a jelly bean and put it in my mouth,

Pick up a jelly bean and put it in my mouth,

This color rhymes with **shoe.**

Pick up a jelly bean and put it in my mouth,

Pick up a jelly bean and put it in my mouth,

Pick up a jelly bean and put it in my mouth,

This color rhymes with **stink.**

Additional verses: Replace bolded words to continue the song.
For example, *This color rhymes with **fellow.***

♫ Yummy Jelly Beans

(sing to the tune of "Alouette")

Yummy, yummy,

Pretty jelly beans.

I love to eat them every day.

If I say that I like **jello,** you know that I like **yellow.**

If I say that I like **jink,** you know that I like **pink.**

Yummy, yummy,

Pretty jelly beans.

I love to eat them every day.

If I say that I like **jite,** you know that I like **white.**

If I say that I like **jurple,** you know that I like **purple.**

Yummy, yummy,

Pretty jelly beans.

I love to eat them every day.

If I say that I like **jorange,** you know that I like **orange.**

If I say that I like **jack,** you know that I like **black.**

Additional verses: Replace the bolded words with other colors. Substitute /j/ for the first sound in each color or add /j/ if the color begins with a vowel. Invite students to say the color word. For example, *If I say that I like **jed,** you know that I like **red.***

Spring Phonemic Awareness Songs & Rhymes © 1998 Creative Teaching Press

(See Syllable Graph activity, page 79)

Clap Your Name

(sing to the tune of "If You're Happy and You Know It")

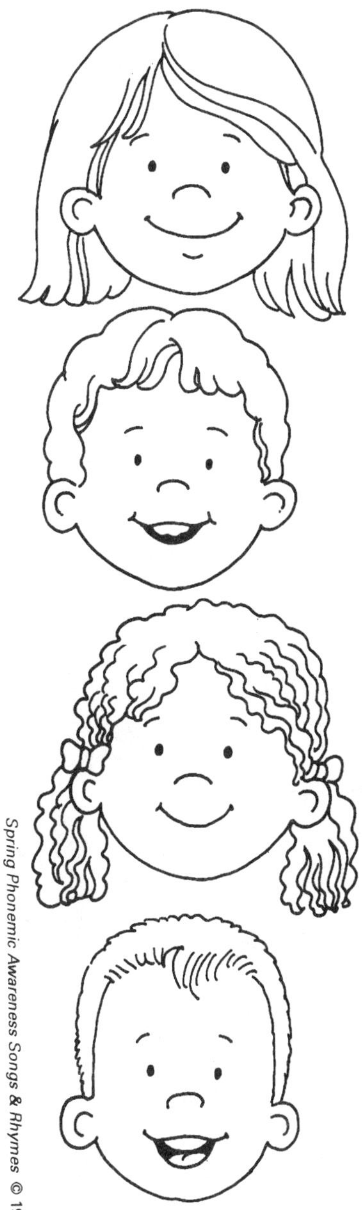

If your name has 1 part, clap your hands.
If your name has 1 part, clap your hands.
If your name has 1 part,
Then clap with all your heart.
If your name has 1 part, clap your hands.

If your name has 2 parts, stomp your feet.
If your name has 2 parts, stomp your feet.
If your name has 2 parts,
Then stomp with all your heart.
If your name has 2 parts, stomp your feet.

If your name has 3 parts, tap your knees.
If your name has 3 parts, tap your knees.
If your name has 3 parts,
Then tap with all your heart.
If your name has 3 parts, tap your knees.

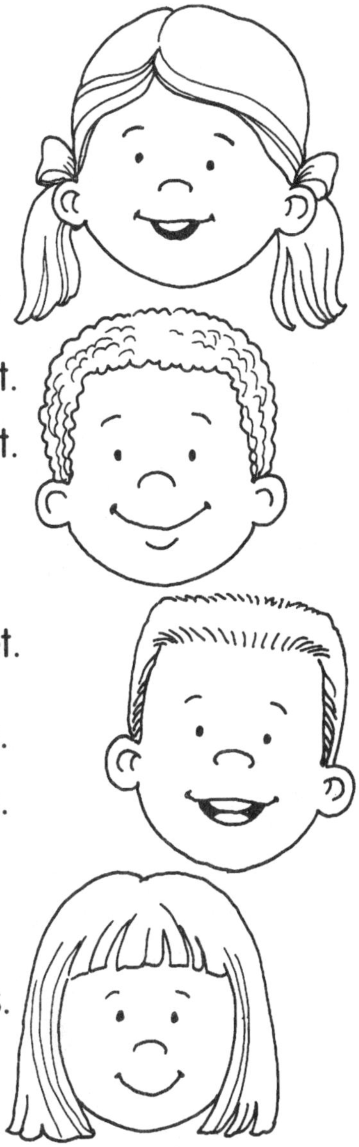

Note: Have students with the appropriate number of syllables clap, stomp, or tap the syllables in their name after each stanza.

Name Game

(sing to the tune of "Dixie")

Cindy loves to sing, you know.
She loves to sing fast or slow.
Cindy-ay, **Cindy**-ay, **Cindy**-ay,
Cindy-oh!

Martin loves to sing, you know.
He loves to sing fast or slow.
Martin-ay, **Martin**-ay, **Martin**-ay,
Martin-oh!

Additional verses: Replace bolded names to continue the song.
For example, *Tommy-ay, Tommy-ay, Tommy-ay, Tommy-oh!*

Spring Phonemic Awareness Songs & Rhymes © 1998 Creative Teaching Press

Color Cues

Syllable Splitting, Phoneme Blending

In advance, cut out large construction-paper egg shapes. Cut some in half and attach the half pieces to each whole with a gold brad. Write a color word on each whole egg with the onset separated from the rime. Write the onset to the rhyming word on the half egg so it covers the onset of the color word. Distribute an egg to each student and have the class sing "Coloring Eggs." Have students hold up their egg when they hear the rhyming word and slide the half egg to reveal the color word.

(Use with "Coloring Eggs," page 65)

(Use with "Coloring Eggs," page 65)

Materials

- "Coloring Eggs" song (page 65)
- construction paper
- scissors
- gold brads

What Will You Pack?

Sound Matching

Have children sit in a circle on a blanket and place a picnic basket in the center. Invite students to each think of something to pack for a picnic that starts with the same sound as their name. Ask students to share what they would pack while singing "Packing for a Picnic." Then invite students to draw on construction paper a self-portrait and the item they will bring to the picnic that begins with the same sound as their name. Add the text _____ *likes* _____. For example, *Peter likes pizza.* Bind the pages into a class book.

(Use with "Packing for a Picnic," page 66)

(Use with "Packing for a Picnic," page 66)

Materials

- "Packing for a Picnic" song (page 66)
- blanket
- picnic basket
- construction paper
- crayons or markers
- bookbinding materials

Picnic Lunch for a Picky Bunch
Sound Matching

In advance, collect food wrappers from student lunches and pictures of food from magazines or food ads. Write on separate large construction-paper sheets each letter of the alphabet and *ch* and *sh*. Display the food wrappers and pictures. Give each student a page. Ask students to find food items that match their sound. Invite students to glue the pictures and wrappers to their page. Students may also draw other food items that begin with their sound. Bind the pages together. Encourage students to continue to bring wrappers to add to the class book. Use the book as a resource while singing "Picky Eaters."

(Use with "Picky Eaters," page 67)

Materials

- "Picky Eaters" song (page 67)
- lunch wrappers (chip bags, fruit roll-up wrappers, granola bar wrappers, etc.)
- magazines or food ads
- scissors
- large construction paper
- glue
- crayons or markers
- bookbinding materials

Our Picnic Picks
Sound Matching

Write on sentence strips the names of each food item from the "Picnic Lunch" song and use Wikki Stix to divide each word. Draw or cut out pictures of each food item. Place the strips and pictures in a pocket chart and invite students to match the picture to the word. While the class sings "Picnic Lunch," invite volunteers to put the words and pictures in a paper lunch sack for a "picnic." For additional practice, repeat the activity with additional food words and pictures.

(Use with "Picnic Lunch," page 68)

Materials

- "Picnic Lunch" song (page 68)
- sentence strips
- Wikki Stix
- food pictures
- pocket chart
- paper lunch sack

Feed the Hungry Thing

Phoneme Substitution

Read aloud *Hungry Thing*. Give each child a photocopy of the Hungry Thing reproducible to decorate and glue on a paper sack. Help students cut a slit for a mouth on their Hungry Thing. Invite students to draw pictures of foods on small paper to feed their Hungry Thing. While singing "The Hungry Thing Goes on a Picnic," invite volunteers to hold up their pictures and have the

class substitute the initial sound with an agreed-upon sound. Then, invite the volunteer to feed their Hungry Thing. Continue with other students. Send the project home with the song on the back for the children to share with their family.

(Use with "The Hungry Thing Goes on a Picnic," page 69)

Materials

- "The Hungry Thing Goes on a Picnic" song (page 69)

- Hungry Thing reproducible (page 93)

- *Hungry Thing* by Jan Slepian and Ann Siedler (Scholastic)

- crayons or markers

- glue

- paper sacks

- scissors

- small pieces of paper

Food Fit for a Frog

Syllable Counting, Phoneme Counting, Phoneme Segmentation

Give each student a blue construction-paper "pond," a few small brown construction-paper "logs," and several green poker-chip or dried-pea "frogs." Ask students to name an insect that a frog might eat. Then have students place a log on their pond for each syllable in the word and place a frog on each log for each sound in each syllable. For example *mosquito* would be represented by three logs for the three syllables (mos-qui-to) and the first log would have

three frogs (/m/ /o/ /s/), the second log would have two frogs (/k/ /ee/), and the third log would have two frogs (/t/ /o/). This activity helps students visualize the segmenting process.

(Use with "Little Green Frog," page 70)

Materials

- "Little Green Frog" song (page 70)

- blue and brown construction paper

- green poker chips or dried peas

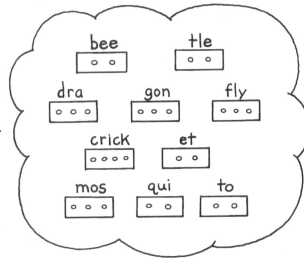

Mmm . . . Jelly Beans
Rhyming

Materials

- "Jelly Beans" song (page 71)
- resealable plastic bags
- jelly beans

In advance, fill resealable plastic bags with one jelly bean of each color. Pass out a bag to each child. While singing "Jelly Beans," invite children to eat the rhyming-color jelly bean.

(Use with "Jelly Beans," page 71)

Pretty Jelly Beans
Phoneme Substitution

Materials

- "Yummy Jelly Beans" song (page 72)
- construction paper (various colors)
- scissors

Cut out construction-paper jelly beans in various colors, write the color word on each, and distribute them to students. Invite students to hold up the correct color while singing "Yummy Jelly Beans."

(Use with "Yummy Jelly Beans," page 72)

Syllable Graph

Syllable Counting

Write each child's name on an index card and glue the student's photo to the card. Write the numbers 1–4 on index cards (one number per card) and place them in the top row of a pocket chart. Invite students to sort the photo name cards according to the number of syllables in their name and place their card in the appropriate column.

(Use with "Clap Your Name," page 73)

Materials

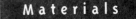

- index cards
- student photos
- glue
- pocket chart

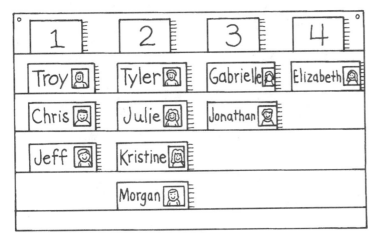

Add an Ending

Phoneme Addition

Sing "Name Game" with your class. After singing the song several times, ask students what sound they want to add to their name. For example, if they choose *ing*, the class could sing *John-ing, John-ing, John-ing, John-oh!*

(Use with "Name Game," page 74)

Materials

- "Name Game" song (page 74)

> Sarah-onk, Sarah-onk
> Sarah-onk, Sarah-ay!

♫ Bugs in My Garden

(sing to the tune of "Are You Sleeping?")

I see bugs, I see bugs,

In my garden, in my garden.

What kind of bug do I see?

Listen first, then blend it with me.

I see a **/b/ /ee/ /t/ /l/**.

Yes, a **beetle**.

I see bugs, I see bugs,

In my garden, in my garden.

What kind of bug do I see?

Listen first, then blend it with me.

I see a **/w/ /o/ /s/ /p/**.

Yes, a **wasp**.

I see bugs, I see bugs,

In my garden, in my garden.

What kind of bug do I see?

Listen first, then blend it with me.

I see a **cat-er-pil-lar**.

Yes, a **caterpillar**.

Note: Have students use two fingers on their wrist to tap the phonemes
or syllables and then blend the word.

Additional verses: Replace bolded phonemes and words to continue
the song. For example, *I see a **but-ter-fly**.*

Spring Phonemic Awareness Songs & Rhymes © 1998 Creative Teaching Press

♫ Here Come the Bugs! ♫

(sing to the tune of "Mary Had a Little Lamb")

Little **bees** go buzzing by,

Buzzing by, buzzing by.

The little **bees** go buzzing by.

/b/ /b/ /b/

Little **flies** go flying by,

Flying by, flying by.

The little **flies** go flying by.

/f/ /f/ /f/

Little **ants** go crawling by,

Crawling by, crawling by.

The little **ants** go crawling by.

/a/ /a/ /a/

♫ Insect Parade ♫

(sing to the tune of "This Old Man")

This little **bee**

Sings **/b/** songs.

He sings **/b/** songs all day long.

With a **bick-back-baddy-back**

Sing his insect song.

He wants you to buzz along.

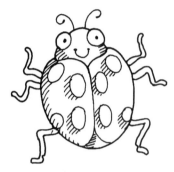

This little **fly**

Sings **/f/** songs.

He sings **/f/** songs all day long.

With a **fick-fack-faddy-fack**

Sing his insect song.

He wants you to buzz along.

This little **cricket**

Sings **/cr/** songs.

He sings **/cr/** songs all day long.

With a **crick-crack-craddy-crack**

Sing his insect song.

He wants you to buzz along.

Additional verses: Replace bolded phonemes and words to continue the song. For example, *This little **ladybug** sings **/l/** songs. She sings **/l/** songs all day long. With a **lick-lack-laddy-lack** sing her insect song. She wants you to buzz along.*

We're Going on a Bug Hunt

(sing to the tune of "The Bear Went Over the Mountain")

We're going on a bug hunt.
We're going on a bug hunt.
We're going on a bug hunt.
What do you think we'll see?

We might see a **but-ter-fly**.
We might see a **but-ter-fly**.
We might see a **but-ter-fly**,
Flying high in the sky.

We might see a **spi-der**.
We might see a **spi-der**.
We might see a **spi-der**,
Spinning a lovely web.

We might see a **bee-tle**.
We might see a **bee-tle**.
We might see a **bee-tle**,
Crawling on the ground.

Note: Have students clap out the syllables for each bug name.

Who's Got the Bug?

Sound Matching, Phoneme Segmentation

Materials

- insect puppet or stuffed animal
- music

Have children sit in a circle. Pass an insect puppet or stuffed animal around the circle while music plays. When the music stops, the child holding the "bug" says a word that begins with the same sound as the bug's name. The other children must pay close attention to the word because they need to tap their knees as they separate each sound in the word, and then they will need to say a new word when it's their turn.

(Use with "Bugs in My Garden," page 80)

Bug Helmets

Phoneme Substitution

Materials

- "Here Come the Bugs!" song (page 81)
- Bugs reproducible (page 94)
- crayons or markers
- scissors
- sentence strips
- glue
- die-cut letters

Invite students to decorate and cut out one bug from the Bugs reproducible. Have students glue their bug to the center of a sentence strip to form a headband and glue on a die-cut letter that corresponds to the bug's initial sound. Invite students to wear their headband as they sing "Here Come the Bugs!" Invite each "bug" to "fly" in turn during the song.

(Use with "Here Come the Bugs!" page 81)

Catch a Bug!

Sound Matching, Phoneme Substitution

Fill a butterfly net with pictures of different insects and/or plastic insects. Have students sit in a circle and invite one student to choose an insect from the net. Have the student name the insect and tell the beginning sound. Invite the class to sing "Insect Parade" and substitute the insect that was chosen. Then pass the net for another student to choose.

(Use with "Insect Parade" page 82)

/b/
butterfly

Materials

- "Insect Parade" song (page 82)

- butterfly net

- pictures of bugs (from magazines) and/or plastic insects

Hunting for Bugs

Syllable Counting

Sing with your class "We're Going on a Bug Hunt." Ask students what they think they might see on a bug hunt and list their responses on chart paper. Have the class clap the syllables in each bug name. Invite each child to glue two small cardboard tubes together and then paint them to make binoculars. When the binoculars dry, hole-punch each side and tie on yarn so students can wear them on their bug hunt. Then, take your class on a walk around the school to search for bugs. When you return to class, add to the list the names of the bugs the class saw and clap out the syllables.

(Use with "We're Going on a Bug Hunt," page 83)

Materials

- "We're Going on a Bug Hunt" song (page 83)

- chart paper

- small cardboard tubes

- glue

- paint and paintbrushes

- hole punch

- yarn

Seed Package

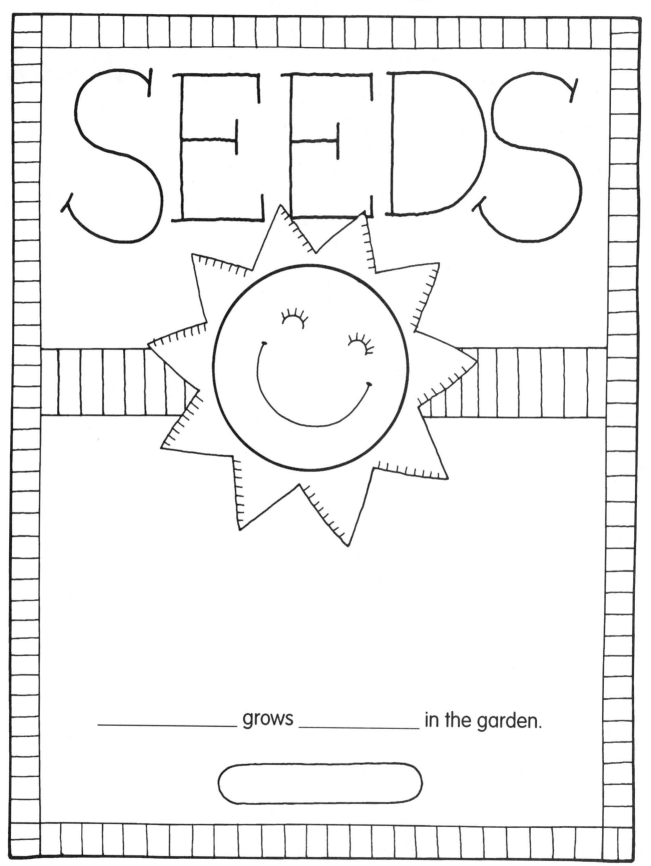

_____ grows _____ in the garden.

Spring Phonemic Awareness Songs & Rhymes © 1998 Creative Teaching Press

Barn

Farm Animals

Spring Phonemic Awareness Songs & Rhymes © 1998 Creative Teaching Press

Animals

Deep Sea Picture Cards

Beach Picture Cards

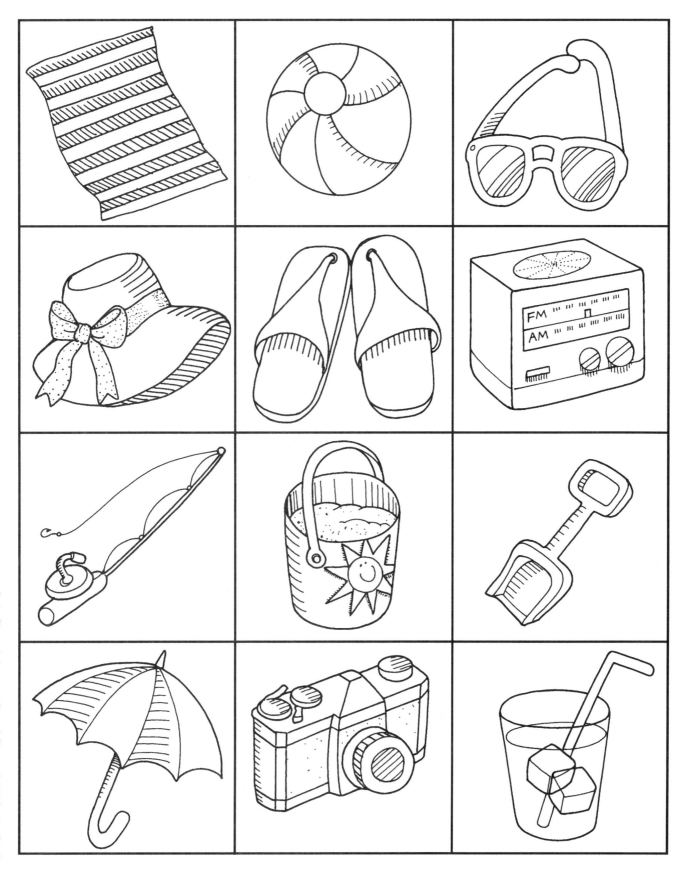

Spring Phonemic Awareness Songs & Rhymes © 1998 Creative Teaching Press

Baby Animal Picture Cards

Spring Phonemic Awareness Songs & Rhymes © 1998 Creative Teaching Press

Hungry Thing

Bugs

Spring Phonemic Awareness Songs & Rhymes © 1998 Creative Teaching Press

Phonemic-Awareness Index

♫ *Song Title*

♫ *Song Title*